Diary of an Almost Cool Boy

Book 1

B. Campbell

Copyright © B Campbell 2014

D0720856

Dedication

To all the Almost Cool Boys and Girls out there.

Stand tall…you don't have to be in the "Cool Group" to be a wonderful person.

Saturday

Snap!

Followed by a terrible grinding noise…as a shower of sparks cascade off the axle of the go-kart. The go-kart then spins off the very steep hill through the long grass and weeds to end upside down against a chain-link fence.

Sounds bad? It gets worse. See, that's my go-kart and I'm sitting in it upside down watching some ants excitedly scamper up the stems of the weeds. They probably think they have just found the best source of food since the dinosaurs died. Hopefully I have bad news for them.

I hear a voice, "You okay son?" It's a track safety marshall. "I'm okay thanks, but can you get the cart off me please?" I reply. My Mom and Dad taught me the value of manners, after all I don't want my rescuer to think I'm ungrateful and go off to help some other crashed kid. The marshall carefully tips the kart over and helps me out of it. He gives me a quick check over and says, "You were lucky kid, not a mark on you." *Sorry ants, looks like I'm off the menu.*

Just then my parents arrive. Well, actually Mom arrives first and Dad about 5 minutes later. Mom is a fitness instructor at Hercules Gym and Dad is a real estate salesman, so that is why Mom arrived first.

Actually Dad is the reason I'm here. Dad likes to tinker with things, you know, like taking the washing machine apart when it doesn't work (then it never works again) or doing his own car servicing.

My Dad

So when Dad heard about the go-kart derby on Johnston's Hill…he entered me. Now some kids bought go-karts and some kids have mechanically gifted Dads who built the go-karts. I have a Dad who is a real estate salesman who tried to build a go-kart. So that's why I crashed and that's why Dad is in big trouble with Mom.

Oops! Almost forgot my manners, I haven't introduced myself. Everyone calls me AJ…no not really. ☹ My name is Arthur James Brewer. I wish people would call me AJ or even Art, but everyone calls me Arthur. I think it's because my Mom always introduces me as Arthur and insists that nobody shortens it.

As a gym instructor, Mom is strong looking, has a very loud voice and is used to people following her instructions. Yes, Anna Brewer is a woman used to getting her own way.

Dad, well…Dad's very different. Easy going, a constant smile on his face and always looking out to sell some property. I blame Dad for my name, his name is Basil. So I think he chose my name so he didn't have to suffer a bad name all alone. Dad nearly always wears a tie, business shirt and long pants. He is fond of the expression, *clothes make the man*, which is why I always try to go clothes shopping with just Mom.

I have a sister and her name is Jane. I'm sure you've noticed that Jane rhymes with pain, that can't be just coincidence. I think the universe was trying to warn us. Jane the pain is 17. She is easy to recognize, there is always a phone glued to her head.

My younger brother is Taj. Yes, I know…why did it take until child number three before my parents became cool and creative with names. Taj is only 6, but going on his favorite activity – he is already set on a future career path. Yes indeed, it looks like he is going to become a professional nose picker. He does it all – the pick and flick, the pick and chew and even the two fingers and two nostrils at the same time. Gross! Mom says he will grow out of it, but in the meantime I use LOTS of hand wash.

My family is rounded off by a crazy parrot called Bella. Bella absolutely loves Mom! And we also have a scruffy little dog called Snoopy.

Anyway, now that you know me…welcome to my life.

Monday

It's back to school for the first day of the school year. I like school, don't get me wrong. I love holidays, but school is important. School lets me meet new kids, I get to play with my friends at lunch time, it fills in the time I'm waiting for new X Box games to be released and sometimes I even learn some things.

I go to Chester Heights School or CH as the kids call it (even my school has a cool name). CH is an old school, so old that both my Mom and Dad went to it when they were kids. The scary thing is that the principal hasn't changed since my parents went to school! His name is Mr. Brown. Mr. Brown is tall, permanently grumpy and let's just say – he spends much more time at the dessert bar than he does at the salad bar. Worst of all, sometimes he says, "Arthur Brewer, you remind me so much of your father." Dad never seems to want to come anywhere near school, so I guess Mr. Brown's memories of Dad can't be good.

Mom drops me off at the school gate. The giant, bright yellow Hummer is already attracting quite a bit of attention, but as Taj and I walk away from the car Mom bellows out in her gym instructor voice, "Go get 'em Brewers!" Then she waves farewell along with a double blast of the Hummer's earsplitting horn. Not quite the low-key arrival for the first day that I had hoped for.

As soon as we are inside the gate I start to walk faster trying to leave Taj behind. It's so hard to look cool when you have your little brother following along like a mini me. Mom always insists on a fresh haircut for the start of the year and of course Taj and I both got the same style. The hair-cuts are really cool, if you were joining the army. Not to swell on it, let's just say the hair-cut is about as far away from the One Direction look as possible, while still having some hair. To complete the picture, Taj and I have matching backpacks and matching shoes. In the same school uniform the only way you can tell us apart, is that I'm bigger and Taj has his finger up his nose.

Finally I arrive at class. As cool as I am about returning to school, even I feel excited about my first day in Grade 6. The teacher, Mr. Adams, is new to the school so we don't know what to expect. At first glance it seems promising, he is quite tall and has a nice smile.

Mr. Adams instructs us to come into the room and tells us that we can choose where we want to sit. Last year our teacher made us sit in alphabetical order and I was stuck between two of the cool girls, who wouldn't even talk to me.

I quickly grab a desk next to my best friend Mike

Smythe. Mike's been my best friend since I started school. He has a heart of gold, kind to everyone and always looks on the bright side of life. The desk on the other side of me is empty. I guess I'm not the most popular kid in school. Mike and I kind of stand alone in *no man's land.* Somewhere between the cool kids, the sporty kids and brainiacs.

Mr. Adams interrupts my sharing of my go-kart story with Mike. He tells us to quickly unpack our books and other gear. From what I've told you about my Mom you probably realize that she is one very organized person, so you can imagine when it came to purchasing my school equipment she did a fantastic job. My school bag contained enough gear to see me through to university.

My gear was so tightly packed in, that my bag was jammed solid. I put my hand in and grabbed some books and tugged. Nothing. I tugged harder, nothing moved. I tipped my bag upside down and shook it. A few sandwich crumbs fell out, but nothing else. Mike holds the bottom of my bag while I grabbed the top of my books and on the count of three…we both pull. Well that sure works! The books start to come out, Mike falls backwards, flipping the bag in the air. My desk and me get covered in a downpour of flying books. But not just any books, but an amazing collection of books covered in bright orange contact. Mom thought it would be a good idea to make sure all my books stood out so I wouldn't lose any.

The class erupts into laughter as I shrink into my seat.

Cedric Crackster is a bully. Cedric bullies me, Mike and pretty much everyone else. A tall, pale faced kid with busy blonde hair and a permanent mean look on his face, Cedric is my worst enemy. Of course he has to make a smart comment at lunch time about my orange books. "Did you mommy write your name on your books when she was making them so pretty," he sneered. Well actually she did, but I wasn't going to tell him that! Instead I blurted out a very lame, "My Mom and I both happen to like orange." Cedric and his little gang of followers walked away laughing.

CEDRIC IS A BULLY

The first day finally ends and I wait out the front of the school for Mom. Then I see Dad's ford sedan come chugging down the street. It stalls at the stop sign and then he takes ages to park across the road. Did I tell you that my sister Jane is learning to drive? That's who is behind the wheel. Fancy giving her a learners permit, have they not seen her drive on X Box. I jump in the back seat and put my seat belt on. Taj is running towards the car, he sees our sister and stops with a look of horror on his face. "Hurry up Taj, " calls out Dad. He looks scared, but jumps into the back seat next to me. He does his seat belt up and checks it twice.

That's when I notice Dad has a crash helmet on, I'm hoping it is just his silly sense of humor. I say, "Hey Jane, where's my crash helmet?" She gives me a death stare that would frighten Darth Vader. And so starts a long and very scary trip home. Several cases of whiplash later we stop in the driveway. Pleased to be home, Taj and I hope out and kiss the ground. Jane snarls at us. I kiss Mom and run to my bedroom. There are two reasons for this...one is to do my homework and the second reason is to get away from my sister as quickly as possible.

My sister
Jane the PAIN!

After dinner I go to bed early. The first day back at school is always so tiring. More importantly I know I need a good night's sleep because during the school term, Mom gets everybody up at 5am to do our fitness routine.

Tuesday

The beeping of the alarm interrupts the pleasant dream I was having about Cedric being abducted by aliens. Mom starts blowing her whistle until we are all assembled at the front door. She looks as fresh as a daisy. Dad leans against the wall half asleep. Taj looks keen as only a 6 year-old boy can and Jane is still trying to strap her phone to her wrist. Me, I'm a little sleepy, but I like the running part because I actually quite a good runner.

Mom leads us on a slow jog to the park where we do some stretches. Then Mom and Dad head off to run 5km, while Jane and I do 3km and Taj a mere 2 km. Mom worked out a circuit at the park so that even though we are running different distances, she can still see all of us. She says this is important so that she can make sure we are all safe, but I think it's so she can check that we are keep running. After Dad struggles in last (his face is purple and he is wet from head to toe in sweat) we all head home for a half hour of pilates and yoga exercises.

My Mom - Very Fit

After breakfast Mom drops us at school as the gym she works at is only around the corner. I do the usual and bolt to leave Taj and head to my classroom. At the room I'm greeted by a strange sight. Cedric is wiping off the whiteboard for the teacher. Then Cedric goes around tidying up the shelves. This is not the Cedric we all know.

Usually the most helpful thing he does is to go home at the end of the day.

I go and sit next to Mike who is already at his desk. "What's up with Cedric?" I ask. Mike doesn't know either, but he tells me that before they came into the room that Cedric made him give him his homework so that Cedric could copy it. When I asked why he gave it to him, Mike told me that Cedric said if Mike didn't hand over the homework he would regret it later. "No way Mike, we're not letting him get away with this, we'll tell the teacher," I urged.

We went to the front of the classroom and waited patiently to see Mr. Adams. He finally looks up from his computer and asks what we want. Mike and I had already decided that I would do the talking as Mike is quite shy. I try to explain to Mr. Adams how Cedric had forced Mike to let him copy his homework. Mr. Adams stares at us for a moment and then turns and looks at Cedric who is still cleaning up.

He calls Cedric over and explains our accusations. Cedric pulls his best innocent face and says, "No Mr. Adams, I would never do that, these two are always trying to cause trouble." Mr. Adams thanks Cedric and tells him to go and sit down. Then he turns to us with a disappointed look on his face. "Boys I'm very disappointed in you both," he says. "How dare you try and get such a nice helpful boy like Cedric in trouble with such an obvious made-up story. You both have lunch-time detention." As we walk dejectedly back to our desks, Cedric gives us a big smile.

Wednesday

Another night of pleasant dreams, this time a terminator came back from the future and took Cedric away. The dream probably was because most of yesterday Mike and I talked about how to get even with Cedric.

After excising with my family and breakfast has been gulped down, we head off to school. It looks like being a hot day so I grab the new water bottle I bought last weekend. It's in the shape of a cute character, I've never seen one like it. Mom said it would be good as it wouldn't get confused with the other kids' water bottles. The thought of drinking someone else's spit is so gross!

In class, Mike and I try to avoid any contact with Cedric. That's not too hard as he sits two rows back and to the left of me. Mr. Adams has just begun the first lesson of the day. When the principal, Mr. Brown, enters the room with two students.

The students are a boy and a girl, although my focus is drawn to the girl. She has long blonde hair and the biggest eyes I've ever seen. I feel Mike's elbow hit my ribs, "Stop staring," he whispers in my ear. I blush bright red and mumble, "I was just wondering who they are." "Yeah sure," replies Mike.

Mr. Brown speaks to Mr. Adams and then leaves alone. Mr. Adams then introduces the two new students. "We have two new students joining us today, Julia Cameron and Hawk Jones, I know you'll all make them feel welcome." That's when I first look at the boy. Hawk, now that is a cool name. Hawk is without doubt a pretty tough looking, broad shoulders and bulging biceps. His hair in in a mohawk style that is starting to grow out and he has a mark on his nose that suspiciously looks like a hole from a nose ring.

"Choose an empty desk and sit down," instructs Mr. Adams. Both kids look around surveying for empty desks. Julia's eyes seem to come to rest on the desk next to me, then she starts to walk towards me. My heart starts thumping in my chest, I stop breathing and I look down. I steal another glance and Julia is almost at the desk next to me. I look at Julia and smile, she smiles back. Wow, the cute new girl is going to sit next to me! Thump, suddenly from behind Hawk slams his bad down on the desk next to me. Julia looks slightly surprised and then turns to the left and sits at the other end of the classroom.

Julia

To Hawk I say, "You're not sitting there, MOVE NOW!" No I didn't really say that, but I wanted to!

I actually said, "Hi, I'm Arthur and this is Mike." He replies, "Hawk" and fist pumps with both of us.

Mr. Adams recommences the lesson and for about half an hour he has us working flat out. The phone rings and Mr. Adams answers it and is soon involved in some conversation about his lunch order with the canteen. Like most of the class, I take the opportunity to stop working. Feeling thirsty I pull out my water bottle and have a long drink. I hear some laughter coming from behind me and Cedric's voice, "Look at Iggle Piggle boy!" I ignore Cedric and have another mouthful wondering what garbage Cedric is on about now. The laughter spreads around the classroom and I suddenly realize people are looking and pointing at me.

"Look he's got an Iggle Piggle water bottle!" calls out Cedric. I realize he is talking about my water bottle. Mike is staring at me with a look of horror on his face. I quietly ask him what is Iggle Piggle and he quickly explains how it's a character on a TV show for little kids. He tells me that my water bottle is in the shape of Iggle Piggle. Suddenly my water bottle no longer looks cute, but more like a deadly weapon against any coolness I might have hoped to have.

Cedric continues to throw insults at me. Hawk turns around and says, "Hey dude, that's my little sister's favorite show and I always watch it with her and I think it's cool. So...enough okay!" Cedric looks stunned. I whisper, "thanks" to Hawk. He just smiles. The room quietens just as Mr. Adams finishes his phone call. Oblivious to the drama that just occurred, starts on his next lesson.

When we finally finish and get to go out for

lunch I find myself walking next to Julia, the new girl. She nudges me with her elbow to get my attention and then half pulls out of her bag an identical Iggle Piggle water bottle. "Sure glad you got thirsty before me," she whispers with a smile. Life at school looks like getting a lot more interesting with Julia and Hawk around.

Saturday

With the school week over, I look forward to just relaxing and playing some X Box. No such luck though, Mom has invited some lady called Pam over for afternoon tea. Apparently Pam is new to the area and Mom met her at the gym. So you know what that mean…adult visitor = hours of house cleaning. Mom sees herself as more of a supervisor, she makes a list of jobs for us all to do. However, Dad's at work, Jane's at her part-time job at McDonalds…which leaves Taj and me. We get to do lots more jobs to make up for Dad and Jane the Pain.

Supervisor Mom finds out my way of putting away my laundry was to push all my clothes under the bed. She tells me to put them away neatly, so I quickly pile them into my cupboard and manage to slam the door shut before they all fall out again.

Sweep, mop, dust….. I'm beginning to feel like Cinderella. I whinge to Mom about Taj not doing his share. She tells me to stop being such a "princess" (I must have said how I felt Cinderella out loud) and then she grabs one of Jane's tiaras and puts it on my head. She thinks she's funny, so I keep it on (parents have to have a laugh sometimes).

Taj and I bake some cookies, half chocolate chip

and half honey cookies. With Taj's nose picking habit, I make sure he washes his hands thoroughly before we start. We actually work well as a team and quickly have the mixtures prepared. As I prepare the trays for cooking, out of the corner of my eye I see Taj's finger up his nose. "No!" I yell. Taj panics and rips his finger out of his nose. To my horror I notice his fingertip has a green booger sticking to it and as his finger is pulled away from his nostril the booger flies off towards me and the bowls of mixture. It all happens very quickly. Flying through the air and landing somewhere. I can't find it. It couldn't have reached the honey mixture. But there is a definite possibility that it could have landed in the chocolate chip bowl. That bowl was still being mixed by the mixer, so if it went in there...it was lost forever. I scan the kitchen bench but the lost missile is nowhere to be seen. No trace of it in the honey bowl either. It had to have landed in the chocolate chip bowl. But I can't see anything as I go through it with a fork.

Obviously there is only one thing I can do...make sure I don't eat any of the chocolate cookies! I spoon the mixture on the trays and place them in the oven.

Mom asks me to do one last job, take the rubbish out to the bin. Yeah, nearly free! Just as I reach the door to take the rubbish out, the door bell rings. I open the door and there stands a lady with blonde hair and big blue eyes. Alongside her stands a younger version of her, obviously her daughter. It's Julia from school!

"Hi," says the lady, "I'm Pam Cameron, your Mom invited me over." "This is my daughter, Julia." I just stand there looking shocked. Both Pam and Julia seem to be staring at the top of my head. "Can we come in?" asks Pam. I just nod, that's when the tiara falls off my head. I quickly pick it up and stammer that it is not mine, it's my sister's. Julia laughs, "Perhaps you should get your own, it really suits you." Thankfully Mom arrives and takes over while I slink away into the kitchen.

After a few minutes Mom calls Taj and I into the lounge room. Mom introduces us to Pam and Julia and both our Moms have a good laugh about how Julia and I are in the same class and they didn't know. Julia and I just stand there looking awkward. Then Pam comments on how similar Taj and I are. Mom quickly pulls out her favorite photo album to show how similar we were when we were babies. Pam and Mom ooh and aah over the photos while Julia looks over their shoulders. I hear Pam say, "What's this photo?" Mom explains how when I was younger, Jane used to dress me up as a princess. She continues on saying that I used to run around the house pretending I was a princess. I am speechless and my face goes red enough to add to global warming! Julia comments, "The way he was wearing that tiara when he answered the door, he must still like dressing up...unless that is his own tiara." She gave me a cheeky, teasing look and started to laugh. They all did. Mom to her credit takes the blame for the tiara, but blows it by saying, "Okay Cinderella, go and get those cookies you baked."

I stomp off into the kitchen to get the cookies that Mom must have taken out of the oven when I was answering the door. As I place them onto the serving plate I remember my suspicions about the choc chip ones...do they have Taj's secret ingredient? Mom and Pam are adults, so they are used to eating gross stuff, but there is no way I'm letting Julia eat one of the chocolate cookies. She'd never want to be my friend if she found out.

I carry the plate into the lounge room, making sure the choc chip cookies are on the side closest to my body. I go to Julia and offer her a cookie first. She asks what types they are. I suggest she tries a honey one, telling her they are delicious. She starts to reach for a honey one when suddenly she changes her mind saying, "Yum choc chip cookies are my favorite." I jerk the plate out of her reach and say, "No, have a honey one." She again reaches for a choc chip and I jerk the plate away again. Some of the cookies spill onto the floor. Mom uses that voice, "Arthur just put the plate on the table and go and clean up that mess."

As I return from the kitchen, I hear her apologizing about me, something about me beginning that awkward stage. How embarrassing! I clean up the mess and say goodbye as I have to go to my room and finish an assignment and stay there until I am 30 (didn't actually say that last part). About an hour later I hear Pam and Julia leaving and wonder what other damage Mom has done to my reputation.

Wednesday

The first two days of the week have flown past. The dynamics of the class have slightly changed. Hawk has been approached by the various groups of "cool" kids, but seems content to hang out with Mike and me. Julia hasn't mentioned her visit to our house to me or more importantly…to anyone else. She has made friends with Brainy Barbara Barnes, our class genius, and some of the other nice girls in our class.

Cedric has been his usual painful self. Today we had sports after lunch, so most of the boys went into the toilets to change into our sport's uniforms so we wouldn't waste time during the lesson. There I was, in the cubicle changing, I put my bag with my sports clothes off the cubicle door and when I take off my uniform pants I drape them over the bag. While I'm pulling my uniform shirt over my head I hear a rustling noise, then some laughter. I get the shirt clear off my head just in time to see my uniform pants and bag disappearing over the top of the door. The laughter continues as I hear someone running out of the toilet block. Now I'm stuck in the toilets with only my shirt and underpants. I creep out of the cubicle and peer out the toilet block door. There lying in the middle of the walkway is my bag and pants. Just off the walkway sits a group of girls and Julia is one of them. Julia is the closest to the door, but she is facing the other way.

I duck back away from the doorway and consider my options.

One - Stay in the toilet and wait till someone comes in and ask them to grab my gear. Risky – I could wait a long time and someone outside might take my stuff.

Two – Sneak out in my undies and grab the bag and pants. Risk – total embarrassment!

Three – Call out to Julia to get my stuff. Risk – embarrassment.

Then a fourth brilliant option comes to mind. I have a thick black marker pen in my shirt pocket, I'll write a message on a toilet roll and roll it out to Julia. I quickly compose a short message asking for her help.

After about 5 minutes I manage to wrestle a toilet roll out of the toilet roll holder. I start my message on it with: *Hi Julia*, and move onto the…*please, please help me* part. I re-roll the toilet roll and aim a gentle roll towards Julia. My aim is good and my hopes soar. I haven't rolled it hard enough and the roll stops short of reaching her. As I watch, hoping Julia will turn and notice the toilet roll, a large bird walks over to the roll, grabs it in its beak and flies off.

Frustrated, I spend another 5 minutes freeing a second toilet roll. I repeat my message and go back to the doorway. Julia and her friends are still there, so I roll the toilet roll again, but harder this time. Beautiful! My roll is perfect, a straight line heading towards Julia's back. The roll is just about to hit Julia's back when some little kid comes running past and kicks the toilet roll, sending it out of my view.

I stomp back into the toilet again and pull out another roll. It's the last one. I rewrite the message for the third time. At the doorway I take careful aim and roll the toilet roll with all my might. Success! It hits Julia in the back and she spins around with a surprised look on her face. She picks up the roll and appears to be reading my message. She looks towards the toilets, so I stick my head out a bit further and wave. Julia puts the roll down and walks over to my gear and throws it through the doorway. Her parting comment is, "I thought Cinderella only lost her glass slipper."

I quickly dress so I can race outside and thank her. Fully dressed with my bag over my shoulder I walk outside. "Arthur Brewer, get over here!" booms Mr. Brown, the school principal. I've found 3 toilet rolls lying on the ground with your name on them. I take vandalism and littering very seriously. There will be NO sport for you today young man and you can have 3 lunch-time detentions as well." I try to explain, but Mr. Brown won't listen. "Did you write your name on these toilet rolls or not?" he yells. I can't lie, but confess that I did, so Mr. Brown turns and walks me off to his office. Every time I try to explain he tells me he is not interested in hearing my lame excuses.

Mr Brown

On the way we walk past Cedric. He sniggers, "Good to see you are out and about Brewer, I heard you lost something."

Friday (2 weeks later)

My chance for revenge finally arrives. Mr. Adams gave us a lot of homework this week. He also announced he would be checking that everyone had done it, as lately quite a few students hadn't bothered to do it. In fact, he said that anyone who didn't finish their homework would receive 2 lunch detentions.

So as luck would have it, that morning Cedric was running late and all the kids he normally intimidated into letting him copy their homework were already in the classroom. Cedric never did his own homework…which was certainly unfair. Cedric's face lit up with hope when he saw me coming. "Brewer," he snarled, "Have I got a deal for you! Give me your homework to copy and I won't bash you." Normally I would just say no and face the consequences, but today I saw my chance for revenge.

I agree to let him copy and tell him to hand on while I get my book out. While Cedric is distracted getting his own book, I open my book to the homework of about 3 weeks ago and quickly change the date to today's date.

Cedric snatches it out of my hands. "Is this it?" he asks. "That's my homework," I reply (well I didn't lie, it is my homework, just not this week's). Cedric quickly and somewhat messily copies it and tosses my book back to me.

I follow Cedric into the room and sit at my desk. After calling the roll, Mr. Adams comes around to check our homework. All is good until he reaches a smiling Cedric. When Mr. Adams realizes Cedric's homework isn't this week's, he just assumes Cedric has tried to trick him. Mr. Adams goes ballistic. Cedric doesn't get 2 detentions, he gets a whole weeks worth.

At lunchtime Mike spreads the story of how I tricked Cedric, I get a lot of high 5's from the rest of the class.

Saturday

On Saturdays some people play a sport, some people fish, some people relax and read a book. Me, well, I prefer to participate in a life-threatening adventure activity. That's right, going with my Mom and sister on another driving lesson.

We take Dad's ford, even Mom's not crazy enough to let Jane drive the hummer. Mom drives us out to a quiet area and then swaps seats with Julia. Mom has a different style of teaching driving compared to my Dad, it involves a LOT of yelling. Jane seems to relate well to this style and after a while starts to yell back. It makes for quite an interesting spectator sport.

Things are going really well. Mom has taken us to a quiet industrial area with almost no traffic. Jane drives around for about 15 minutes and nothing is damaged and nobody is hurt. Then Mom has a great idea, Jane should practice parking. Mom chooses some parks outside a factory. Simple parks, the ones you drive into and back out of.

Under Mom's guidance, Jane successfully parks several times. Then Jane utters the words, "This is easy." Jane drives around the block and comes in for another park. "Too FAST!" screams Mom.

In the back seat, I just scream. Jane panics and instead of braking, she accelerates. The front of the car pushes into the chain-link fence in front of the park. There is a loud scraping noise and the roar of the car engine before we lurch to a halt when the engine stalls. Silence. Then Mom says in a much quieter voice, "I might drive us home now."

As we head home, I break the tense silence with, "I can't wait to tell the kids at school that I survived a car crash." "NO!!!!" screams Mom and Jane in unison.

Monday

Mr. Adams gives us a huge Geography assignment to do on a country. The assignment has many aspects to it and the finished product has to be presented in PowerPoint on a computer.

A lot of my classmates look worried to be faced with so much work, but not me. I've seen this assignment before…my sister Jane did the exact same assignment a few years ago. You're probably thinking, *how do you know*. Well, Jane got an A for her assignment and she still talks about it. I was made to sit and watch it with the rest of the family. Mr. Adams must have borrowed the idea for the assignment from the teacher in the next class, Mr. Higgins, who used to teach Jane.

Fortunately, even though Mom can be very like a drill sergeant, she also has a soft mushy side and a lot of storage space. In the spare room she has kept and labeled virtually every piece of schoolwork that any of her kids has done. When I get home after school I go straight to the spare room and start searching. It doesn't take long before I find a USB memory stick in a zip lock bag labeled Jane's China Project. Gotcha!

Over the next two weeks, all my friends go into hibernation as they spend all their spare time trying to get the assignment done in time. Mr. Adams even gives us 2 weeks off normal homework so that we can devote the extra time to our assignment. For me, that is 2 weeks of extra time to play X Box, watch TV and go skateboarding.

Friday

Today is **A Day**. The day the assignment is due. The day I get an A.

Mr. Adams collects all our USB's so that he can run our presentation through his computer and data projector. He then informs us that he'll show the sample assignment he showed us earlier to remind us of what he expects for an A standard presentation.

I lean across to Mike and say, "I don't remember him showing us an example." Mike whispers back, "He showed us the day you came late to school." I remember that day, it was the day Mom turned our trip to school into another driving lesson. Jane's driving skills turned our 10 minute trip into a 25 minute nightmare. I'm not worried about missing the sample assignment anyway as I know my assignment is an A standard.

While Mr. Adams starts to show the sample assignment, I start to finish some drawings in the back of my math book. Suddenly the sound of some music snaps my attention to the whiteboard. It's the same music Jane used. My eyes bulge from my head as I realize that Mr. Adams' sample assignment is Jane's actual assignment. He must have borrowed it from Mr. Higgins who must have kept it because it was so good.

My mind races!!!! What can I do????

I wait until Mr. Adams finishes explaining to get an A, the presentations have to be of a similar standard to this one. I walk slowly out to his desk and ask if I could have my USB back as I just realized that I forgot to add something and I could give it back to him tomorrow. He replies how fantastic it is that I'm still trying to improve my work, but to be fair to everyone else he can't do that.

It takes 3 days until Mr. Adams gets to my assignment, but only a few hours after that for him to arrange an interview with my parents. No one is happy, except for Jane, who is so proud that her work is so highly regarded. I'm grounded for two weeks and I have to do two assignments instead of one. Mom and Dad threaten me that if my report card isn't good…they'll put me in Summer School.

I feel bad about using Jane's assignment now and not just because I got caught. Mom and Dad spoke to me about it and I realize that taking credit for work that I didn't do is wrong. After all, that is what Cedric does all the time and I never want to be like him!

Monday

Lunch breaks are really fun now with Mike, Hawk and myself hanging out together. Sometimes Julia's group of friends joins us too. Julia is such a nice girl, she never has spoken about that embarrassing visit to my house or the toilet roll note. Our little group of friends is always happy and supportive. I can feel my confidence growing all the time. It's like Mom always says, "Who your friends are…helps to define who you are."

We need that support to continue to keep Cedric under control and off our backs. Cedric has a nasty habit of taking our things, like rubbers, pencils, sharpeners and highlighters. We know he takes them because he flaunts them in front of us. If anyone claims he has their stuff he just says, "Prove it!" He always carefully removes any name tags and claims the stuff is his. He has this oversized pencil case, where he keeps his stolen loot.

Today Hawk revealed to us that he has been keeping a secret. Apparently his Dad is a very rich and successful I.T. guy, specializing in anti-hacking and anti-virus systems. It gets better…Hawk is eventually going to take over the business and his Dad has taught him all he knows to prepare him for his future. Hawk is usually home-schooled, but his family let him come to our school for "socialization". We told Hawk how we thought he was some type of tough kid with the mohawk and the hole that looked like a nose piercing.

Hawk laughs and explains that the haircut is finally starting to grow out. He did a TV ad for his Dad's business and he had to get his hair cut that way. The hole in his nose was from when he had a mole removed to make sure it wasn't a skin cancer.

And this is the best one. His name isn't really Hawk! It's actually Hank!

His parents did all the enrolling online and never actually came to school. So Hawk got into the school's computer system and changed one letter. Hank became Hawk and suddenly Hank became much cooler.

When Hawk and I were alone he told me one more secret that he wasn't ready to share with the rest of the group yet. He rolled up the leg of his pants to reveal an artificial leg. I'm shocked and ask how did it happen. He told me a story about a mean and nasty shark that bit it off.

Then he started laughing and explained that he was born the bottom part of his leg just wasn't there. That's why he looks so strong. Hawk has really defined biceps from working out to get stronger and using crutches to rest his leg. He didn't want to tell everyone else because he said that people treat him differently when they find out he only has one leg.

Wednesday

Yesterday Cedric had a really busy day, adding a lot of other kids' stationery to his pencil case. So last night, Hawk and I hatched a cunning plan.

Hawk has a really cool Lego ruler that you can snap apart and put back together again. Most importantly the end of the ruler is attached to a key-ring with a little oval picture frame with a photo of Hawk inside it. Hawk carefully glued the lid down so that the photo couldn't be taken out. The key-ring also doesn't come off the ruler.

Just before lunch Hawk made sure that his ruler was on top of his desk in plain view. When he returned to his desk after lunch, the ruler had vanished. Part A – complete. Now for Part B.

Mr. Adams is at his computer again, as we do some quiet reading. In the silent room, the ding of an incoming email notification on the teacher's computer sounds loud. I peek out from behind my book and see a puzzled look on Mr. Adams face. He stands up and moves to the front of the room.

"Attention class, I've just had an email form the principal. He has instructed me to do a pencil case check on all students immediately. So please stand and empty your pencil cases onto your desk." Hawk gives me a nod and wink, as we tip out our cases. Everyone except Cedric that is. Mr. Adams notices and asks Cedric to empty his pencil case. A cascade of pencils, pens, rubbers and a Lego ruler flow out of Cedric's case. "Hey, that's my ruler," calls out Hawk. With everyone's focus on Cedric's treasure trove, suddenly kids start recognizing their property and calling out, "That's mine!"

Cedric stands, with his head down, as Mr. Adams supervises the children reclaiming their stolen property. The last we see of Cedric is as he walks off to Mr. Brown's office. After school I high 5 Hawk and say, "Brilliant, that fake email you sent to Mr. Adams worked so well."

That really was the last time we saw Cedric at school. His parents were so upset when they heard about his stealing that they transferred him to another school.

Bullies 0 verses Good Guys 1

Saturday

The thing about Jane's driving lessons is that you never know where the danger is going to come at you.

Take the last lesson for example. One minute I'm minding my own business, eating the last of the block of chocolate that Jane had left in the fridge. When out of the blue, Jane bursts into the room, sees me popping the last piece of chocolate into my mouth and has a total meltdown. You know, the teenage girl thing when they start out yelling and end up crying and slamming doors.

I did the usual little brother thing when Mom came in…a bit of denial (I didn't know it was your chocolate), a bit of teasing (well I can understand why you are so upset, that chocolate was so good) and finally the retreat – where I sneak out of the room quietly and hide.

First two worked really well, but the sneaking out was foiled when Mom insisted we all sit down so we can all have a talk. This is parent code for they talk and the kids listen. Anyway, Mom sorts it out…so nobody dies (me – the one in the most danger) and nobody is crying (Jane).

Mom decides a nice drive will be a great idea. So Taj and I climb in the back. Dad is at work still so he won't be coming. Jane gets in behind the wheel and Mom is in the front passenger seat.

Jane is driving quite smoothly and fairly slowly, so I'm feeling comfortable and start to look around. That's when I notice that everyone is extra friendly today. I see people in other cars waving to us, some even honk their horns. Mom and Jane are too focused on the driving and don't seem to notice.

After a while I realize that people aren't waving but actually pointing. I try to tell Mom but Jane laughs it off saying, "They are probably pointing because our car has such a beautiful driver."

Finally when we stop at a red light, a car pulls up beside us and signals us to put our window down. Jane does and we hear the people in the other car yell out, "There's an ipad on your roof!" After a slight hesitation as we digest what we just heard, Mom rips open the car door and looks on the roof. She lets out a squeal and grabs the ipad, which sits just above Taj's door. "Taj you left the ipad on the roof! Sometimes you are so irresponsible!" screeched Mom. With an "oops" Taj tries to disappear into the car seat. Mom explains that the grip on the cover probably stopped it from falling off. "Lucky for you Taj," she snaps. "Although don't expect to use the ipad anytime before you become an adult."

Looks like I'm sitting in Number One position as Most Popular Son with Mom at the moment.

I decide to make the most of my improved status and ask Mom if I can have an ice cream. Mom agrees and directs Jane to the street where the ice-cream shop is. There is only one park left and it's between a beautiful sky blue BMW and a white Audi Convertible. Jane starts to move into the parking space. She is super nervous and slightly crooked. She slams on the brakes and says, "No way, I can't park between them!" Sensibly Mom agrees and they both jump out to swap sides.

Now I don't think I have mentioned how Jane is really short and Mom is quite tall. Whenever Jane drives she has to move the seat a lot closer to the steering wheel. This means that Mom can barely fit into the driver's seat and once in she has to slide the seat back.

Normally this is no problem, but this time Jane has left the car running. I guess Mom felt under pressure because the owner of the beautiful BMW was walking to her car.

Mom quickly jumped in and that was when it all went horribly wrong. Jammed into the narrow space between the seat and the steering wheel, Mom's foot got stuck. And worse still, it was stuck on the accelerator! The car jumped forward and scraped down the side of the previously perfect BMW. But don't worry, our cars dramatic acceleration stopped when the front of the car hit the palm tree on the footpath.

Final Result: BMW is no longer perfect, it has a red stripe down its side, our car has a dinted bumper and bonnet and the BMW lady looks in shock, her mouth is wide open and tears are streaming down her face.

Mom was SO embarrassed! She apologized a million times. After swapping insurance information we drove home in our battered car.

The trip is fairly silent, Mom is thinking – *how will I tell Dad*; Jane's mostly thinking – *Yes, I didn't do it!*; Taj, well Taj is 6, he doesn't think. Me, well I look at Mom's face and I'm just glad I didn't ask if we were still going to get an ice cream.

Friday (several weeks later)

Cross Country Day

This is the first year we are able to compete in the school cross country race. I feel really excited because thanks to Mom, I'm pretty good at running. My friend Mike is a great runner. He assures me that girls like sporting heroes…although I'm not sure how he knows this. But perhaps if I can win or even do well in the race, Julia might notice me a bit more.

The starting gun fires and Mike really takes off. He is so fast I don't think I'll be able to catch him. The track winds around the oval, out through the back fence of the school, up a small hill and then back through the school's side gate. We have to do 3 laps of the course.

At the end of the second lap, I can't see Mike, he is so far ahead. I'm doing well too. I'm starting to lap the slower runners. The girls from my class are spectating because they have finished their race earlier. Every time I go past they give me a big cheer. I can see Julia cheering extra loud for me. I can't help it, as soon as I see them I speed up and sprint past them. Maybe Mike was right.

Mike my best friend

When I reach the bushy area, where the girls can't see me, I slow down a little and try to catch my breath. It is half way through the last lap, at the bottom of hill, I find Hawk sitting on the ground clutching his leg. I can't just run past my friend, so I stop to check that he is okay. The bottom part of Hawk's artificial leg has come loose and he can't walk on it.

He can't let anyone else help him or they'll find out about his artificial leg. Hawk has a special tool that will tighten the leg in his bag, back outside our classroom. If I finish the race and then go and get the tool, almost certainly some kid or a teacher will arrive and try to help Hawk and discover his leg. Friends come first. I decide to take a short cut over the fence to go and get Hawk's tool, then race back and then try to finish the race. I think I'm currently in third place.

I run as fast as I can. On the way I sprint past Mr. Brown, who calls out to me, but I pretend I can't hear him. I get the tool from Hawk's bag and help him to tighten the leg. Then I take off to finish the race. I run as hard as I can and finish in fourth place. I just missed out on getting a trophy, but fourth place receives a ribbon, so that is okay.

About 10 minutes later Hawk finishes and gives me a great big smile. The Deputy Principal gives out the trophies to the first 3 places and he is about to pin a ribbon on my shirt when Mr. Brown arrives on the scene. "Don't give that boy a ribbon! I saw him cheating and taking a short cut!"

Everyone looks on in shocked silence. Mom and Dad are frowning at me, Julia is looking at the ground and Mike's mouth is wide open in surprise. "Hang on," calls Hawk as he hobbles to stand beside me and before Mr. Brown. "Arthur wasn't cheating by taking a short cut. He was getting a tool to fix my artificial leg," he insists while rolling up the leg of his pants. "He actually ran further because of me, otherwise he would have finished higher."

The whole crowd starts clapping and cheering for me. Mom starts crying, Dad is beaming and so is Julia. Mr. Brown apologizes to me as he pins the fourth place ribbon on my shirt.

I turn to Hawk who shakes my hand as I say, "But Hawk, now everyone knows about your leg." He smiles and says, "Friends come first, remember." Mike comes up and shakes my hand and Julia gives me a high 5.

Life is good!

Hey Almost Cool Kids, can you please leave a review to help me sell more Almost Cool Books?

Some more books you will love…

6878407R00037

Printed in Germany
by Amazon Distribution
GmbH, Leipzig